The Tale Unknown: Part I

Written and Illustrated By Drew Ray

The Tale Unknown – Part I

By Drew Ray

Dedication

Behold *The Tale Unknown*!
This book is lovingly dedicated to my wife, my children, and my wonderful family and friends. Without your love, support, and unwavering belief in me, none of this would be possible. Thank you for being exactly who you are — you inspire me every single day. I love you all to the moon and back.

A Note from the Author

The Tale Unknown is a deeply personal passion project.
I've written many poems over the years, but this collection represents the heart of my journey — and the height of my craft so far. These poems were born in a time of personal darkness, and in writing them, I found light. They became my compass.

In these pages, you'll follow a Captain and his crew on a voyage toward the impossible — a story about persistence, courage, and the belief that even when the odds are stacked against us, we can still chart our own path forward.

This is only the beginning. *Part II* and *Part III* are in the works, but the story has waited long enough. I'm proud to finally share it with you.

With gratitude and hope,
Drew Ray

The Fisherman's Son

Amongst the men who work the docks

Lived a fisherman as good as any

He'd bring his son down near the rocks

Tell him tales of lands with resources of plenty.

The boy grew up listening to his father's tales

Filling his imagination with what could be

On the boy's sixteenth birthday

They set sail lands scattered across the sea.

They ventured out beyond the reef...

Leaving their landlocked Island with a mountainous surround.

Winds behind them, grins showing teeth.

They set course incompetent of the dangers around.

The boy's mother,dead from labor, but this day he lost his father to the sea. The father's hand caught in rope, the winds strong providing no favor. The ship rocked, the waves grew, the father taught the boy to sail while constricted he... Told the boy to change course toward the calmer reef. As the boy turned a wave crashed and the father was flung beyond the mast. The boy panicked, he must act fast, he let go of the wheel only to find...

His father's neck twisted in binds. As the voice drew soft the father spoke...

"The lands are true... you will be fine... I will see you son on the other side."

As his breath grew faint while the rope did choke, the father reached for his knife and cut the rope. The father fell like any other from his tales...

The sea took another as, tales never fails...

The boy grabbed the wheel with a tear in his eye. He sailed back to shore, his head not high. His life took his mother. No sisters, no brothers. His dreams took his father... So, he chose not to bother the sea any longer.

He devoted his next four years learning many crafts. He learned art and skills he needed to achieve his father's dreams. But he dared not sail any larger rafts. He learned to dig; he learned many things as he sat at taverns to snoop. He learned skills by listening to masters. Till one night he snuck by the pastors. He became a pirate that night with one foul swoop. He snatched his holy grail; he stole the pastor's sloop. His journey starts here on the first of March...

He sought the knowledge in his heart.

He sought to free his mind of guilt.

He knew very well; he'd play his part.

He'd set sail in a month with knowledge he'd built.

He would tell the tale untold

He would tell the Tale setting sail to unknown

That day he changed his name some were told

But he'd be damned not to tell the tale unknown.

Six Lost Souls

One man in a riddle did play on his fiddle. A soft and gentle tune. His siblings could chisel, but he was in the middle of art and singing with the moon. He was the middle child, siblings old some little to his folks he was considered a goon. But he knew many arts from music to charts. He longed for purpose, his talents not worthless. He longed for adventure to give him some pleasure. He is one lost soul, it's true.

Another man tough as nails. He was a forger of rails; he could fix any issue he knew. He would craft fine blades and steel billets he made, becoming the finest swords others drew. His family nonexistent so he was persistent in working on swords and his brew. He was a skilled fighter who crafted alcoholic ciders. He longed for purpose, his talents not worthless. He longed for adventure to give him some pleasure. He is one lost soul, it's true

The next lass was a cook. Her nose in each book, she held knowledge with ease. She could cook and sail, a fishing woman, not male. But she'd hang with the rest as she pleased. She studied the land with pickaxe in hand to find anything useful with glee. She could search all day long just humming her song. She longed for purpose, her talents not worthless. She longed for adventure to give her some pleasure. She is one lost soul, it's true.

One man worked with wood anyway that he could. He would whittle all day you see. He would build where he stood and make repairs as he should. He was stubborn as the devil could be. He's always under the hood. He could make what you wanted to see, he worked dusk till dawn just humming along. He longed for purpose, his talents not worthless. He longed for adventure to give him some pleasure. He is one lost soul, it's true.

One mother of three, all slaughtered, they be. As she mourned her losses alone. Her husband left free, but was lost to the sea. She knew when he left he'd be gone. She started with four, a full life with no bore. Now she's left with their ashes and bone. She knew how to survive alone with her pride. She longed for purpose, her talents not worthless. She longed for adventure to give her some pleasure. She is one lost soul, it's true.

A man, skilled in navigation who walked the whole nation, he walked every last mountain hill. He knew of medicine and could survive with the best of them. He was a doctor prescribing the pills. He could fish, he could hunt. He was the toughest of grunts. He knew so much but still. He wanted much more with the whole world to explore. He longed for purpose, his talents, not worthless. He longed for adventure to give him some pleasure. He is one lost soul, it's true

They were six lost souls we knew!

A Worthy Crew

A long time ago in a shattered land

A boy in search of knowledge did band

A worthy crew, it's a challenge to find

A worthy crew to journey to enrich the mind.

Be it so the boy knew

He'd have to captain the worthy crew.

He distributed notes across his known land

For the brave, the bold, even his right hand.

Only a few were needed to man the ship

Only a few were needed but all needed grit.

His note had a day for sails to set.

Six showed up, six responders was all he'd get;

They scoured town for supplies in mind,

but they knew not the duration of this ride.

The captain wanted to sail seas unknown

in search of seven new lands, felt in his bones.

He knew not if seven lands were true

Based solely on tales of the oceans blue

Overtime, his confidence in the tales

were the drivers and winds behind his sails.

He estimated the journey would last years,

His crew heard of these deathly fears and tears,

but they all had held word true

alas he found a worthy crew.

A Tale Untold

Today we will tell a tale untold

a captain, a pirate, not interested in treasure and gold

a captain, a pirate not curious of what's to conquer

a captain, a pirate in search of land and knowledge to ponder

he was taught as a boy of seven seas by his father

his dreams of curiosity filled with wonder

He knew he had to set sail, be bold.

His goal was to tell the tale untold.

a captain, a pirate dreamed of seven seas and seven lands

a captain, a pirate with five crew members and one trusted right hand,

seven aboard the stolen sloop to set sail

seven in search of truth to unveil

one captain, six pirates, supplies for months, wood and nail

in search of truth in search of pride in this untold tale

seven members destined to reach uncharted land

one captain six pirates one crew together one goal at hand

one crew to sail the ocean blue

one crew unknown to the world till now

We set sail in search of the stories truth

This journey, this epic, this unknown captain, till now

one crew set sale on the ocean blue

one crew unknown to all but me and to you.

Captain's Log Day 1

Today be the day.

Today be the day.

Today be the day to venture beyond the reef

The first of May an adventure beyond belief

I gathered my crew

They're worthy and true

Today be the day.

Today be the day.

I been waitin' four years to overcome these fears.

I been waitin' for ages to fill up these pages.

I gathered my crew

They're worthy and true

Today be the day.

Today be the day.

Musician's Position

There is a prediction that the musician's position may be one of the most important roles at sea.

For it is up to one fine fellow to keep the mood nice and mellow, playing the things he sings.

The style, the tune, must set the whole mood, and tell stories for the others that be.

He plays on a fiddle, he teaches the others to sing, he brings drums and he hums.

Just a ring-a-ding ding.

He boosts morale, and entertains, he's got soul in his veins.

A true pirate this man must be.

He never shies fast, just sitting under the mast, he hums and hums

Just a ring-a-ding ding.

He beats on his drum, sat down on his bum, he hums and hums

Just a ring-a-ding ding.

The tunes come a flowing, a smile he's showing, as he hums and he hums

A ring-a-ding ding.

Captain's Log Day 57

I can't help but think something is out there

It calls me like this fresh salty air.

We been traveling for over a month and a half

I have the feeling in my gut we are on the right path.

Beyond the reef we went

And now we have traveled far.

My crew is nothing but spent

But they perform well above par.

How I miss smelling morning dew

We will find land, me and this crew.

Our boat is locked on course for sure

We will strike land. I feel it evermore.

The wind is heavy, it fills my sails

I know we are close. I feel it, I see it, out in the distance. I feel the land that fulfills me wishes.

I am sure that we will find something worth this journey. I am sure this is true.

My boat is strong, and so are my crew. We will journey along

This ocean blue, we will strike land one day,

It's true.

Smith

The man called Smith, he's much more than a myth.

He manages to fashion fine weapons aboard a ship.

It is true, he created a forge once he climbed aboard.

Standing six foot two, it was blades he knew

He could parry and was

on guard all day long!!!!

He makes it a point,

To tell the whole joint

About his next sword

Made. He was fierce

And he would pierce

With only a gaze!!!!!

He is poised and calm

And works all day long.

He is the best Smith.

He is not to be messed with,

And he will tell you.

He makes it a

point.

Captain's Log Day 117

At night we rest beneath the stars.

We dream of the day we strike land afar.

I know it is close. I feel it in my bones.

My crew grows tired, but their skills be honed.

We fish and we cook, we chart, and we look.

But alas, no land in sight for miles around

So today I chose to fill this book

While my fiddler be playing a beautiful sound.

My right hand has been stuck in the nest, scavenging with eyes, he's truly the best.

My ladies be practicing fighting it's true, they spar till sun sets on the ocean blue.

My blacksmith is fashioning weapons a plenty. To keep from his boredom.

My wood worker is tired but patches holes with the swordsman.

We all stay busy day to day. Along this journey

Surely soon our luck shall be turning.

But till then we will sail along

We will strike land

Won't be long.

Cooked

How many dishes can she make with the fishes?

How many meals? Can she feed a great deal?

It is nothing but her wishes to be the fine misses,

that feeds a crew as bold as this one

She gazes upon her small stove with a mission

When she speaks up you need to listen, she is quiet and humble as any.

She has a small stature but that's never a matter, as she will strike you down with her gaze as she pleases. She works all day making meals, gourmet. But don't be fooled, she will fight when needed. She stands but five foot three, she's tough as they be, just cookin' days in and out.

Almost as tough as the toughest around, our cook is not one to be messed with. She is as fiery as her kitchen. Here are her rules, take a listen. If you try to fight with her, dinner will be missin'. Don't show up late, or you get the small plate. Always smile when she hands you the dish, best not mess with the one who cooks fish. Cause her last rule is don't be a fool. Clean your messes alas she confesses. If you catch her good side she hands you the plate with the dresses.

Make sure the catch of the day is in her lap by noon. She will make sure you eat soon.

She fires up the grill and sharpens her knife for the kill.

Before you know it you hear a smack!

Lunch is served.

Captain's Log Day 153

Sure as day we will make it I swear

I have faith of the fruit this will bare

153 days sailing not a land mass in sight

153 days behind us and so many night

I dream of the day that we strike land

I dream of the day for me and this band

But till then we will sail on

Day in day out, dusk till dawn

Wood and Nail

Wood and nail, wood and nail

Would you hand me the wood and nail?

I take my hammer and repair the ship.

I'm sharp as any aboard this trip.

You hand me the nail

You hand me the sail

And I fix as I wish!

I make it a point,

hammer the joint!

And our ship stays

Afloat. Yes our ship

Stays afloat cause

Of me. Naysayers

Beware or I'll cut

Yah with these

Wood and nail

Wood and nail

I will take you out with wood and nail. I never hesitate, I'm no snail. I'll sever your finger if you dare mess with me. The Smith thinks it's him, but I'm the toughest that be. I was a carpenter in a past life, but now I fix boats. I'm the only thing here makin' this float. If you get too close as I'm workin', just stay careful where you're jerkin', cause it's my hammer that's lurkin'. I'll let out a smirk and hammer the nails through the boards. I'm just dreamin of shores. Waiting for the day we dock. So I can take a look at the trees stare at the stock. Get some more wood so we can still float. Yes I'll fight till my last breath before I let this one fail to float. This is my boat you see!

Captain's Log Day 205

My crew is tired my ship has been ripped

My hands are calloused from a steering grip

We make due each day and each night

We are adventurers and this is our plight.

Could this be all for not?

Should we have stayed, or be glad we did not?

These answers are looming over my head and this crew.

Each day that passes I lose faith that it's true.

Still hopeful till my last breath.

Still hopeful till my own death.

Stoic (the Widow's mantra)

Stoic is the one who endures all to live another day.

Stoic is the one who shows no fear, no pain.

Stoic is the one who lifts up their head, shows face.

Stoic is the one who lives another day.

Captain's Log Day 365

May 1

It has been one year at sea

Day 1

Feels like a blur to me

I....

I....

I....

Can't help but be ashamed of myself

I promised to enrich, to flourish with wealth

I know that my crew is tired it's true

Maybe we die out here

Maybe we're lost

Maybe someday

We won't be,

But now

We are.

Right Hand Man

Beneath the blood-red banner's flight,

Stood always by the captain's might,

A shadowed figure, lean and strong,

The pirate's right hand, all along.

With silvered sword and keenest eye,

He cut the waves and split the sky.

A loyal heart, both fierce and true,

To his captain and their ragged crew.

Through storm and strife, through clash and roar,

He braved the seas, sought every shore.

No treasure gleamed without his hand,

No conquest crowned without his stand.

He knew the maps like the stars above,

Navigating tides with a silent love.

Yet whispers ran from ship to port,

Of secrets in his heart's dark court.

For though his eyes held loyalty's gleam,

He harbored a dream within a dream—

To one day rise and claim the helm,

To rule alone in this lawless realm.

But till that day, beneath the sun,

He served the captain, the chosen one.

A right hand steadfast, never betrayed,

The silent force in the pirate's parade.

Year One

Aboard the ship were supplies for the trip

any hole that rip would be repaired quick

year one fell short

the ship desperate to port

the once optimistic cohorts were begging Cap to abort

year one no results Cap's dreams coming to halt

rations low even the salt

Cap's guilt runs heavy with fault

Till one day it was the second of May

From the nest, shout of "Aye, land ho!" Dear Cap yelled for a shanty to play

land was in sight, the crew prepared for fight,

but to their delight, only small animals in sight

they hunted and gathered charted land while tattered

nothing else much mattered for the land was mastered

No humans were found no camps or towns

Just sweet chirps and sounds for miles around

18 months explored

Enough rations were stored, land charted and more

Cap yearning for more yells out all aboard

year one came and went for six months spent

in a new land which meant the goal had been met

sea one leads to land one all charted all done,

Six pirates and one captain's journeys just begun

one crew set sail towards days a new one crew set sail onto year two…

Captain's Log: Journey Onward

The adventure continues November first, six months into year two

The successful journey proved my dreams to be true

The faithful team, loyal, strong, and bold this crew

We set sails to new lands across the great blue.

Year one brought success. Where will I go in year two.

We will venture to another new land, it's true.

I can't help but think there is more out there for me and this crew

Every day we searched, and searched; nothing but waves of blue.

Our journeyman fill most of their time

Fishing, cooking, sparing, and maintaining the ship

The blacksmith's blades were perfectly crafted

The charter's papers were perfectly drafted

The cook's dishes were always delicious

The woodworker always knocking due to superstitions

The widow had love for blades, she was viscous

And the fiddler would sing, dream, and rhyme

I'm kept busy manning the ship

We traveled so far and made it to land.

We stocked for months of supplies from there

We hunted, and gathered, most everything is aboard.

Except one thing that caught the blacksmith's eye.

Ruby, gold, and emeralds were found in the rocks and sand.

Treasure was something I thought, never dare.

But something the crew said struck a chord.

That we should take the riches, should I?

Pressure, pressure grows from treasure.

Nothing but pressure put on me, no pleasure.

Treasure, treasure beyond what we could measure

Pressure for Treasure

Pressure for sure.

But we journeyed onward, I stuck course

Northeast I assured with no remorse

Waves would crash as storms came and went

Waves fearsome as if devil sent

Four months of storms all hell bent

On making this journey one hell of a time

Crashing against the sloop, sundering rips

But four months past and we struck land two in that time

A rocky looking island is our destination from this four month trip.

Devil's Island

Picture this, a mountainous island, with lava flowing slowly down the jagged rocks, red so deep it's glowing yellows and oranges, reds all showing from multiple spring like volcanoes growing from their depths throwing lava to the sky. Loud bangs and various chants shouting low to high.

Picture this, six pirates, one captain, smiles glowing slowly down the jagged rocks, rips so deep it's slowing, tearing and hinging, the boats showing damage from rocks underneath, blowing holes to their ship, slowing to a halt its time. Loud bangs and various chants shouting low to high.

See, we arrived.

Year two land two we had find

But this one ominous

No promises if

We would survive

The crewmen dock to this land

But it reeks of demons, death, and sand

This one is ominous

Devil sent

It's Devil's Island

Would we survive?

Captain's log day 666

This land appears before me eyes.

Ashes, from raining fire to the skies.

Our crew be tired from this journey

But we've come too far, no way I'm turning

I see lava flowing fiercely from fountainous forests. Through the trees burning, making a fiery fortress. But it doesn't seem we are the first ones to be here. A dock lies in the distance and the hills seem to be screaming. We must prepare for war, we must prepare for anything. I see a burning face carved out of the lava. It resembles nothing of the tales from my father.

I'm terrified, petrified, down right scared. It appears we may have stumbled upon the Devil's lair. The only things I can describe what I'm seeing are dark devilish hellish gleaming rocks in the sky on the ground, but we must port and see what's around.

We are low on supplies. We are beaten. But we'd been sparring so we couldn't be defeated.

I will tell the crew a speech to prep

I will assure them no wrong doings will occur

I will take ownership of this next step

I will tell them what I must, but survival is unsure.

We will dock in an hour

For now I shall rest

I will voice to empower

But this surely be a test

It's February 27th fitting I suppose.

Six hundred and sixty-sixth day of the journey and we are devilishly close to an island of hell. Surely this can't end well. But if we make it this will be one damned story to tell. Let's get to it, let us enter this hell.

The speech

Crewmen hear me. Hear me now! What we see before us is smoke and mirrors. I know we may be scared, but I see something new.

So I ask you,

Do we dare to dream a dreamer's view?

Dazzling skies, rain or shine leave morning dew.

Or do we stay stagnant and take the casual point of view?

That no one is special, not me nor you?

See I dare to defy the mold

To make new visions of stories to unfold.

To deny my heart would leave me cold.

We promised to take to the sea to tell the tales untold

It would give me nothing but purpose, our talents not worthless. I'm but one captain and we are together seven pirates. My pen has been my ship, now let us swing swords to fill our sails. These words shall last and bring you along this trip. We will set sails one morning together and brave the seas no matter the weather. This was the promise we will hold together. Storms, they will pass and new days shall come fast. We will realize the dreams that dreamers dream. We will write the words to new songs and chart new lands. We will sail together seven strong. We will dock today and we will fight along. Let us draw our blades, let us take a stand. Let us take to the dock of this devilish land.

The Intruders I

As our crew preps to dock on Devil's Island we realize they are not alone.

Boats sit at the dock, but they appear damaged and worn down to bone.

Our crew raises the colors, the jolly roger higher than the sky

Our crew raises the sails as if to sneak right by.

We dock this night, light candles and step foot near the lava flowing island.

We expect immense heat but to our surprise the lava is cool to the hand.

The Captain whispers to the crew "split up, three with me, three due east"

If anyone spots something, be not scared and fight any beast.

We are intruders to this land, expect to be treated as such.

Then the crew split up.

The Captain takes the two lassies and the blacksmith. He decides to trek west on the island. This lava is ever flowing, ingrained in the sand. But it does not appear to be heating or cooling just an ever flowing gleaming stream. Cap takes a bottle to attempt to scoop up some of the goo. It's soft, it's luscious, it seems almost gold. This surely is something never seen or told. After scooping up some of the lava a loud noise did brew. Cap is shocked by the glass unphased by the goo. Look, this resource is something fresh, something new. It glows in gold in a bottle to hold. It is passed around to examine, but that sound. It's loud now like a roar or a growl. Take this to the ship I will not stray far. Take this to the ship, then meet me near the post in the distance. Captain starts walking, slowly but resilient. Until a cloud of smoke appears beneath him. Through the smoke there appears a shadow. Cap draws his sword prepared for a battle. A dark faced woman appears through the cloud with glowing white hair and piercing eyes.

Put down your sword, you won't need that here. She says to the captain as she closes in near. She is tall, she is fair but she is haunting as she stares. Without blinking an eye. She tells the captain she is a spirit here. What all you see is not really here. We are all lost souls, we are all predating your trip. Be careful, what you see here is not for the weak. The captain shellshocked utters a phrase, smoke and mirrors this place it's all up in blaze. She tells him it's the land of death every soul lost to the sea ends up here with me. My name is Pandora. This is my land, some call me Lilith some call me damned but regardless you are here but not like the others. You are here but not perished. Ah, your life must be cherished. She draws closer and reaches out her hand showing a box glowing with the same hue as the lava Cap just bottled. You took something from me, you can return it or you can face my wrath. Cap foolishly scoffed and laughed. Smoke and mirrors this land. Smoke and mirrors and sand. You are just a vision I will turn back. She said not before the incision. She touches his forehead with her nail and drew an X marks the spot on him and his crew. A curse is now set on you and your ship, return what you stole or your body shall rip. The cloud fades away and she disappears as Cap faints.

He awakes caught near a blaze a spring volcano shoots near his face. He screams he shouts he looks for his crew but he is now alone beaten and blue. The Cap decides to try and search the land he was stripped of supplies except his compass in hand. He heads east towards the shadows looking for anything in sight. But there is nothing but tight dark paths, no ideas and no light. The captain must be bold; he feels covered in gold. But he was missed by the crew, covered in mist. He could see them in the distance but they couldn't see or hear his screams or his calls.

Pandora did curse him scared with an X above his eyes his crew can't see or hear him, he floats through the skies. He is now ghostly with a hollow shell as a body. He desperately needs to find out how to return to his true state. He feels as if sealed is his fate.

He walks to the crew as they stand over his lifeless corpse. He sees himself dead and the others mourning of course. They take his body to the ship, his crew now clueless of what to do.

They know they should search the island and keep their word true, they must continue for Cap if only they knew. He is following them in the shadows through this hellish place. They scavenge the island with a hellish fast pace.

They search all over and they see nothing but lava and bones on an island full of poor lost souls. But as they walk despite losing their captain the crewmen are piecing together a story of what could have happened.

Cap walks the same path but sees shadows fighting. It's chaos, it's madness, it's downright frightening. Blood being shed from left to right cannons shot and guns aimed to fight. He walks through until he spots someone he knew. His father stands in the distance with a cannon he blew. Cap rushes to greet him, yelling out Dad dad it's me it's true. Dad dad is it really you?

The father pushes the captain down and says listen here kid I have no idea who you think I am. But there's no chance I am your old man. I have no family. I have been fighting for ages. Feels like eons. I've been rattling cages but you should be wary. Nothing here is for you, not with that scar on your head. That scar be true. Pandora has you trapped. That's a matter of fact the only way you get out of this hell is returning her gold.

The captain smiled for he knew that was his old man. He decided to rush to the ship to get the bottle of gold that he stole. Only to find he couldn't lift it. He couldn't touch it. Then Lilith appeared hollow eyed and upset. She says it needs to be returned by your crew. God if only there was some way to tell them, let us check in on the curse that befell them.

TO BE CONTINUED…

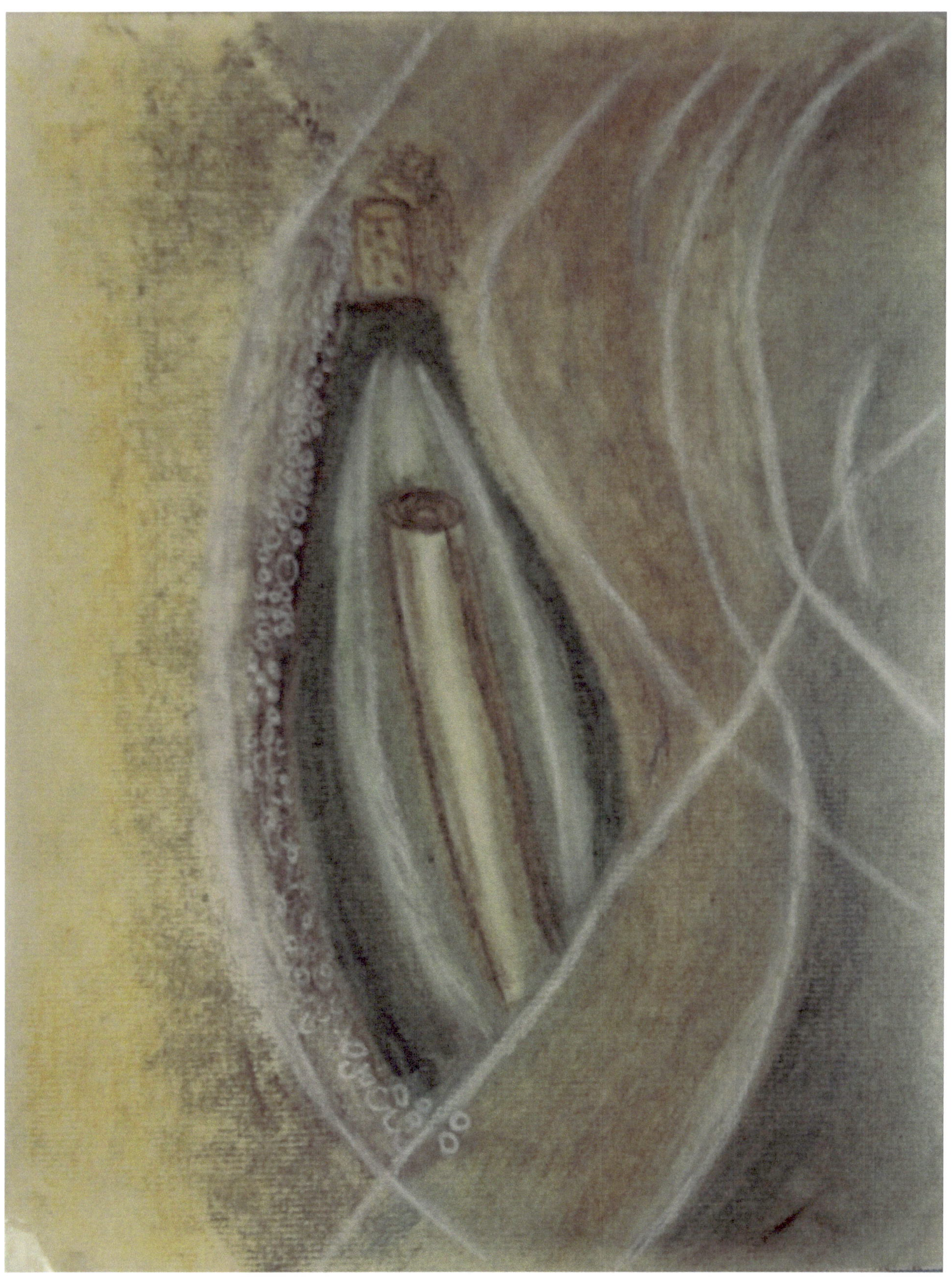

Closing Thoughts from the Author

If you've made it this far — thank you. The Tale Unknown: Part I is only the beginning of a much larger journey, and your time spent in this world means more to me than I can express.

This story was always meant to unfold in three acts. What you've just read is the storm before the calm, or possibly the calm before the storm; The first swing of the compass needle pointing toward something greater. There are many questions left unanswered, and yes — I left you on a cliff. But fear not: Part II is already taking shape, and Part III is close behind.

In the next chapters, we'll dive deeper into the crew's purpose, the mystery behind the Unknown itself, and the choices that will define their legacy. You'll see old faces challenged, new ones emerge, and truths uncovered that even I didn't expect when I first began writing.

So keep your eyes on the horizon. Whether you found this book through a recommendation, a quiet bookstore corner, or a random click online — I hope it stirred something in you. And I hope you'll sail with me again when the next leg of the journey begins.

The remaining pages are empty Captain's Log Journal pages, meant for you to take notes and write your own thoughts about the stories of the Seas. Feel free to send them to me on social media or through my website to stay in touch!

Until then — stay curious. Stay bold.

And never stop chasing the Tales Unknown.

With all my thanks,

Drew Ray

Captain's Log Day:

Captain's Log Day:

Captain's Log Day:

Captain's Log Day:

Captain's Log Day:

Captain's Log Day:

Captain's Log Day:

Captain's Log Day:

Captain's Log Day:

Captain's Log Day:

Captain's Log Day:

Captain's Log Day:

Captain's Log Day:

Captain's Log Day:

Captain's Log Day:

Captain's Log Day:

Captain's Log Day:

Captain's Log Day:

Captain's Log Day:

Captain's Log Day:

Captain's Log Day:

Captain's Log Day:

Captain's Log Day:

Captain's Log Day:

Captain's Log Day:

Captain's Log Day:

Captain's Log Day:

Captain's Log Day:

Captain's Log Day:

Captain's Log Day:

Captain's Log Day:

Captain's Log Day:

Captain's Log Day:

Captain's Log Day:

Captain's Log Day:

Captain's Log Day:

Captain's Log Day:

Captain's Log Day:

Captain's Log Day:

Captain's Log Day:

Captain's Log Day:

Captain's Log Day:

www.ingramcontent.com/pod-product-compliance
Lightning Source LLC
Chambersburg PA
CBHW041134100726

47911CB00003B/126